DEAR DUMB DIARY,

Never do anything, EVER

More of Jamie Kelly's diaries

LET'S PRETEND THIS NEVER HAPPENED

MY PANTS ARE HAUNTED!

AM I THE PRINCESS OF THE FROG?

NEVER DO ANYTHING, EVER

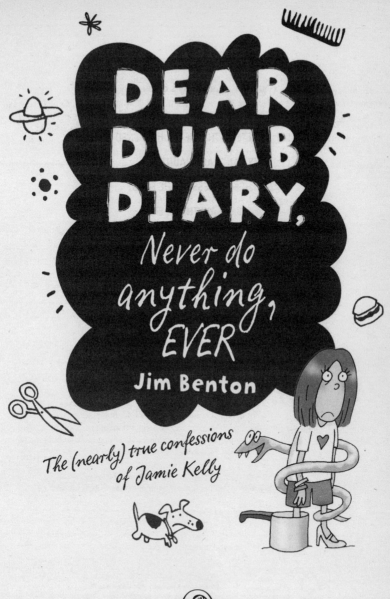

DEAR DUMB DIARY,

Never do anything, EVER

Jim Benton

The (nearly) true confessions of Jamie Kelly

PUFFIN

PUFFIN BOOKS

Published by the Penguin Group
Penguin Books Ltd, 80 Strand, London WC2R ORL, England
Penguin Group (USA) Inc., 375 Hudson Street, New York, New York 10014, USA
Penguin Group (Canada), 90 Eglinton Avenue East, Suite 700, Toronto, Ontario, Canada M4P 2Y3
(a division of Pearson Penguin Canada Inc.)
Penguin Ireland, 25 St Stephen's Green, Dublin 2, Ireland (a division of Penguin Books Ltd)
Penguin Group (Australia), 250 Camberwell Road, Camberwell, Victoria 3124, Australia
(a division of Pearson Australia Group Pty Ltd)
Penguin Books India Pvt Ltd, 11 Community Centre, Panchsheel Park, New Delhi – 110 017, India
Penguin Group (NZ), 67 Apollo Drive, Rosedale, Auckland 0632, New Zealand
(a division of Pearson New Zealand Ltd)
Penguin Books (South Africa) (Pty) Ltd, 24 Sturdee Avenue, Rosebank,
Johannesburg 2196, South Africa

Penguin Books Ltd, Registered Offices: 80 Strand, London WC2R ORL, England

puffinbooks.com

First published in the USA by Scholastic Inc. 2005
Published in Great Britain in Puffin Books 2012
001 – 10 9 8 7 6 5 4 3 2 1

Text and illustrations copyright © Jim Benton, 2005
The moral right of the author/illustrator has been asserted
All rights reserved

Set in 16/18 pt Tarzana
Printed in Great Britain by Clays Ltd, St Ives plc

British Library Cataloguing in Publication Data
A CIP catalogue record for this book is available from the British Library

ISBN: 978-0-141-33585-8

www.greenpenguin.co.uk

MIX
Paper from
responsible sources
FSC
www.fsc.org   FSC™ C018179

Penguin Books is committed to a sustainable
future for our business, our readers and our
planet. This book is made from paper certified
by the Forest Stewardship Council.

*For the teachers we put up with
and the ones that put up with us*

With many thanks to Mary K, who helped out even more
than usual on this one, and the team at Scholastic,
who have inner beauty and outer beauty, but let's not
quibble over the exact amounts here. Thanks to my
glamorous genius editor, Maria Barbo, who actually
chose those words to describe herself, our fabulous art
director Steve Scott, our scrupulous production editor
Susan Jeffers Casel, the magnanimous Shannon Penney,
and Craig Walker, who is Maria's boss, and therefore
required by law to be even more ingenious
and glamorous than she.

This Diary property of

Jamie Kelly

School: Mackerel Middle School

Locker: 101

Phys Ed: Mr Dover

Main Sport: Jumpropery

Worst Sport: Baby Tossing

Main Inner Beauty: Get back to ya on that one

Most Embarrassing Moment: We'd need a lot more paper

ONLY A SUPER
GROSS PERSON
READS ANOTHER
PERSON'S DIARY

SERIOUSLY,
you have a bowl of
TUNA Casserole where your
soul is supposed to Be
if you read a person's
Diary

Dear Whoever Is Reading My Dumb Diary,

Are you sure you're supposed to be reading somebody else's diary? Maybe I told you that you could, so that's okay. But if you are Angeline, I did **NOT** give you permission, so stop it.

If you are my parents, then, **YES**, I know that I am not allowed to call people idiots and dipwads and blondewads and half-wits and turds and all that, but this is a diary, and I didn't actually "call" them anything. I *wrote* it. And if you punish me for it then I will know that you read my diary, which I am *not* giving you permission to do.

Now, by the power vested in me, I do promise that everything in this diary is true, or, at least, as true as I think it needs to be.

Signed,

Jamie Kelly

PS: Angeline, if this is you reading my diary, then you should know that reading another person's diary is a **federal crime**, and a very **ugly** thing to do, and no amount of staggering beauty — inner or outer — can compensate for it.

PPS: Which means that you stand a good chance of being the **ugliest** girl in prison, and if you have ever watched any of those **REALITY POLICE VIDEOS** on TV you know that most of those girls would need an **EXTREME MAKEOVER** just to achieve the delicate good looks of a warthog.

Sunday 01

Dear Dumb Diary,

Isabella and I happened to see Angeline at the store today. Isabella wanted to buy some of that hair-removing foam because her arms are too weirdly hairy. I tried to talk her out of it, not because her arms aren't hairy (because they ARE kind of chimpy), but because little hairless naked baby arms would be way more weird.

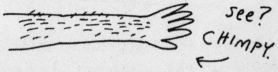

see? CHIMPY. ←

Angeline was sniffing around over by the hair stuff, obviously shopping for whatever secret things she uses to keep her hair all perfect.

As you may recall, Dumb Diary, Isabella is a master of disguise. She quickly grabbed us some sunglasses and hats so we could secretly follow Angeline and see what she bought. (Quick note on disguises: as you're walking, you have to occasionally lower the magazine you're hiding behind so you don't knock over a display of baby-bottle nipples.)

Surprisingly, Angeline didn't buy shampoo or conditioner or colouring gel or hair straightener or unstraightener or anything big like that. She only bought one little item and she carelessly led us right to it. **A BARRETTE.**

It must be some sort of special hair-clip because Angeline, as everyone knows, is beautiful to the point where you know it probably even actually sickens her sometimes to look in the mirror.

But now Her private Barrette Secret is ours!!!!

Ha-ha, Angeline! Let's see how you stack up to me now that I also possess your precious, secret, simple barrette.

BEHOLD!

I would've bought more than one except the store guy wanted me to pay for the magazines I wrecked during the nipple event.

Monday 02

Dear Dumb Diary,

    Okay, these barrettes are not as simple as you may think. I mean, sure, you can sort of pull your hair aside with one, and that's okay, I guess, but Angeline must have some sort of special technique for attaching it to her head, because I couldn't exactly duplicate her results.

I wanted to practise on Stinker's ears a couple of times to get the hang of it, but Stinker is very, very sensitive about his ears and it upsets him to have them touched, so I had to sit on him to do it.

Anyway, I think I finally got it, and tomorrow I am really going to have it going on. Here's a drawing of me having it going on. (I think I may also be all up in that, but I'm not sure exactly what that means.)

PROBABLY JEALOUS

Tuesday 03

Dear Dumb Diary,

Remember Hudson Rivers (eighth-cutest guy in my grade)? I am very sorry to report that he has a vision problem. Not only did he utterly fail to notice the **spectacularness** of **My New Hair Accessory** when he was talking to me at my locker today, but when Angeline walked right past and inflicted **Beauty** upon him he failed to even notice her. I wish I could have enjoyed the moment more, except I felt bad about Hudson's tragedy — I mean, *everybody* notices Angeline.

Angeline had the beauty turned on full blast

At first, I wondered if maybe Hudson just wanted to talk to *me*, and wasn't that interested in Angeline at all. I mean, c'mon, he did write me a poem once. But, fortunately, Isabella was on hand to explain how wrong I was. She says that people who don't notice Angeline have some sort of problem like:

Vision Issue. Perhaps fork-related.

Are only interested in physically ukky people.

Are fossilized or almost fossilized.

If the tragedy is limited to Hudson's eyes, I said that he could just get glasses, and then Isabella flew into this huge crazy rage about glasses and how they destroy your life and how she would do anything to get rid of hers.

When Isabella says she would do "anything", you should believe her. One time when she was five, she physically attacked a mall Santa for not bringing her a panda bear **the previous Christmas**. It was pretty terrifying. When the paramedics finally arrived, he had lost a lot of nog, and was shaking like a bowl full of jelly.

To perform Artificial Resuscitation on Santa, You are required to keep his head under the mistletoe throughout the procedure.

Tuesday and Thursday are my Phys Ed days. Thankfully, it's at the very end of the day, so I don't have to walk around stinkfully afterwards and we can also hear the buses line up right outside the gym, which is a handy way to tell time since the only clock in our gym, like most gym clocks, was broken by a basketball back in 1945.

SMASH

they all probably looked like Abe Lincoln back then

As usual, we ran laps in the gym today, which made me feel like I was going to have a baby out of my left side.

I calmly suggested to Mr Dover that he find something new for us to do as I lay on my back and tried to massage out a cramp that had developed inside the cramp that was inside the cramp in my leg.

He looked at me for a moment, and I think he felt some pity. Or disgust. Anyway, he said, "Okay." I'll bet it's going to be something great!

Wednesday 04

Dear Dumb Diary,

Today, Mom made me gather up old clothes and junk I didn't want any more. She must be giving them to charity or something. It has been a while since I cleaned out the drawers. Here are a few of the items I decided to part with:

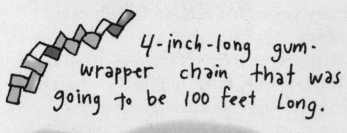

4-inch-long gum-wrapper chain that was going to be 100 feet long.

MAGIC 8-BALL THAT ALWAYS Gives the wrong answer.

Box of Barbies with failed makeovers.

The old clothes made me think back to simpler times, and wonder why I ever wanted to grow up. And then I saw this shirt I used to wear that has this stupid duck in a cowboy hat on it. The main feature of this shirt was the massive permanent chocolate-pudding stain on the front. I wondered how many times Mom had dressed me in that **Big Ol' Pudding Stain** and let me go out in public.

If my future children are reading my diary years from now, here's a tip: if you spill pudding on your shirt, don't tell Grandma. She will let it rot on there until it grows mould or other funky-smelling fuzzy stuff. Tell Mommy Jamie and she will lovingly make Daddy wash it.

And, while I'm talking to **The Future**, here's a little note to myself, in case I am reading this diary years from now when my mom is all super old:

Dear Adult Jamie:

Your mom loves you and did her best raising you, but you're really hot and really rich now anyway. Sure, she made just a few mistakes, and so she should feel good about that because it means that you only have to get even with her for a mere handful of things. Here are a few ideas I had just to get the old revenge ball rolling:

SQUSH SQUIRSH

NO NO

CLean HeR face with a SPITTED-ON NAPKIN IN ReSTAURANTS Like SHe USeD TO DO TO ME

PRUNES ONLY

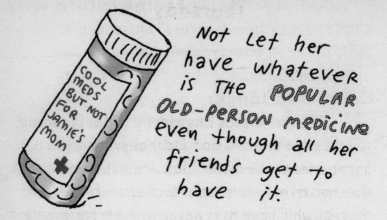

Not let her have whatever is THE POPULAR OLD-PERSON medicine even though all her friends get to have it.

COOL MEDS BUT NOT FOR JAMIE'S MOM

SELL HER GROSS WEIRD OLD-LADY Things OUT ON THE LAWN WHERE EVERYBODY CAN SEE THEM

15¢

35¢
MEDICAL THING

50¢

Thursday 05

Dear Dumb Diary,

You know what Thursday is, right, Dumb Diary? It's **Meat-Loaf Day** at school. (Have I mentioned that before?) Today's meat loaf tasted like **morning-breath-baked-into-loaf-form,** which means it was a distinct improvement over last week's meat loaf.

In Phys Ed this afternoon, Mr Dover (his first name is *really* Ben. Can you believe it?) told us that he took my suggestion to try something new, and we will be starting a month of some new Phys Ed programme called something like **Outward Adventure Outreach Something.** It's supposed to build teamwork, which is when a whole bunch of people work together to do something wrong instead of doing it wrong one at a time.

Teamwork

So Dover began by putting us into little groups of four. Of course, Angeline and Hudson wound up in the same little group because Angeline has some sort of **Evil Power** over the Universe. Margaret was also in Angeline's group. (Margaret is the school pencil-eater, which means that she is the only one whose **number 2 pencils** actually wind up as her **Number Twos**.) Fortunately, Mr Dover made Isabella the fourth member of that group, so at least I have somebody to spy on Angeline and Hudson for me.

My group was me, Mike Pinsetti (he's the nickname king of our school, and he might have a crush on me – YUCK! – and he is a huge human sack of turds), Anika Martin, and **That Ugly Kid Whose Name I Forget** – who I am going to abbreviate as **T.U.K.W.N.I.F.**

PINSETTI   ME   TUKWNIF   ANIKA

OKAY, SO WE'RE NOT EXACTLY THE FANTASTIC FOUR

Our first exercise was called **Trust Falls**. This is when one group member closes their eyes and slowly tips over backwards, trusting their teammates to catch them before they hit the ground.

Isabella has mean big brothers, so her ability to trust human beings has decayed away to nothing. Isabella could no more summon the trust to fall backwards into somebody's arms than she could fall backwards into a wood chipper.

AS FAR
AS SHE CAN
GO

This got her into trouble with Mr Dover because Phys Ed teachers get upset if you don't go all jocky and high-fivey about their little sporty events. Which was good, since it kept me from getting in trouble when Pinsetti cracked his head on the gym floor because I may have been staring across the gym at Angeline and Hudson when I was supposed to be not letting Pinsetti and his trusting head down. But, in my defence, Pinsetti and his head are probably too trusting.

Anyway, Mr Dover switched Isabella with Anika, so now I don't have anybody to listen in on whatever Angeline is saying to Hudson, whose vision seems to have miraculously been restored to normal as far as staring at Angeline goes.

Of course, she did have her barrette artfully embracing one silky ribbon of flawless blonde hair, and Hudson may have been fixated on that alone.

HELPLESSLY BARRETTE-BLIND

Friday 06

Dear Dumb Diary,

Angeline is doing some sort of Walk-A-Thon for charity this weekend, and she asked Isabella and me to sponsor her.

This is where we donate a dime for every mile she walks. I know, it **sounds** good, but Angeline doesn't just walk in a straight line. Eventually, she turns round and walks back. If she just kept walking and walking, I'd give her a hundred bucks. But she said it's for some sort of amazing cause like **Sending Stuffed Animals Full of Candy to Hungry Toddlers in Wheretheheckistan.**

I don't know. We said okay.

← Pure niceness and sensitivity →

Later, as we considered Angeline's sacrifice and her willingness to volunteer her time and effort for people she doesn't know who live millions of miles away, we had to admit . . .

Angeline is super stupid.

Saturday 07

Dear Dumb Diary,

    Dad dropped me off at the salon today. This is supposed to be one of the best hair salons in the whole city, and the stylist, Collette, is really and truly from France or some place where she graduated from the greatest hair college in the world. Collette usually cries at the end of our appointments, and lots of times she asks me to leave through the back door, but I think she has to keep seeing me because they made her take some sort of oath back at hair college. It's like how doctors can't just walk past you if you're in an accident. And, let's face it, my hair is bleeding to death on the sidewalk.

    I really didn't even need a haircut, but I asked her to put in the barrette. She spent a long time dealing with it and couldn't get it to work. She said my hair was rejecting the barrette like a transplanted organ, but, if I wanted, she could phone a **Barrette Consultant** of hers to talk her through the procedure.

I was pretty psyched about this, since, if it's somebody's job to be an **ON–CALL BARRETTE CONSULTANT**, they're going to know techniques that even Angeline hasn't heard of!

When Collette returned, she said that she couldn't get hold of the consultant. The consultant's mom said that the consultant was out getting sponsors for a Walk-A-Thon tomorrow, but we could try back later if we wanted to.

That means the mystery consultant could be only one person . . . Like I was going to give Angeline the satisfaction!

probably some kind of secret experimental atomic barrette

BARRETTE HOT LINE

I told Collette that I had just remembered that our school had a policy against barrettes because a month ago a girl was innocently nodding her head and her barrette flew across the room and clamped round the neck vein of some nasty blonde girl and she went unconscious and now barrettes are illegal and they're considering putting some limits on scrunchies as well.

CLOMP

I know. I know. It was a pretty stupid lie. But I don't have the deception abilities Isabella has in moments like this. I'm just not in touch with my **Inner Evil** the way Isabella is, and I know that I am probably a huge disappointment to her because of it.

OH, Isabella - I'll try to be worse - really I will

OK... she's probably NOT **THIS** upset

Sunday 08

Dear Dumb Diary,

I discovered Mom's latest sinister plan. She wasn't **donating** my old clothes. She was having a **GARAGE SALE**. When I woke up this morning, Mom had put mountains of our junk out in the driveway.

Have you ever seen a mom preparing a garage sale? Fussing and figuring if she should ask two cents or three cents for the warped Tupperware lid?

Mom! Please! Say three cents and then we can buy that yacht we've always wanted.

Isn't it better to just let people suspect that you have crappy junk than to haul it all out in the driveway and prove it to them?

DELIGHTS That Await You AT GARAGE SALES

Large box of
Nasty old shoes
to nicely
accessorize your
Hobo Outfit

very affordable
washing-machine
door

Old toys no longer
considered legal
for CHILDREN

Our garage sale, however, featured an even bigger, uglier surprise: this huge group of people started parading past our house. When I got up to see what was going on, I realized it was that stupid Walk-A-Thon. I even saw Angeline and a bunch of other kids and parents from my school walk right past my actual house. I'll bet she was the one who chose this route. I was so mortified that they were going to see my old gross stuff for sale in the driveway that I locked myself in my room and refused to come out **For As Long As I Lived.**

OUR STINKY STUFF

If you ever decide to do something **For As Long As You Live,** you're going to find out that this takes a lot longer than you thought it would when you said it. And by dinner I was ready to put aside my mortification for the fragrance of pizza that was wafting in from downstairs.

And get this: Mom gave me forty-five bucks from the sale of my old junk! At least something good came from the **PUBLIC SALE OF SHAME.** I guess I have to give her credit for scheduling our garage sale for when the Walk-A-Thon was going by. And maybe Angeline didn't even notice my gross stuff.

OKAY. MOMS ARE GOOD FOR CERTAIN THINGS. LIKE...

They give you cash!

they seem to enjoy cleaning

It's fun to laugh at How they dressed 15 YEARS AGO

PHOTO ALBUM

Monday 09

Dear Dumb Diary,

Angeline had her picture in the town paper today, and the whole school saw it because they put the article up in the lobby. It would be bad enough if she was just looking adorable and non-sweaty, but they happened to take the photo in front of *my house*, and you could actually see my **Big Ol' Pudding Stain** in the background.

Amazingly, nobody said anything. Evidently, Angeline had forgotten I lived there.

Isabella and I gave Angeline the money we had pledged the other day. Angeline walked ten miles, so it only came out to a buck apiece. **How much could she possibly have raised?** Five bucks? Six?

Angeline asked us if we wanted to pledge her next charity walk, and we said that we had already committed to a different charity.

Pretty fast thinking, huh? It's only because I've heard my dad use it about a jillion times when people call us at home for donations. He's got a bunch of great excuses to not fork over money.

WAS JUST ROBBED BY TEENS

ACCIDENTALLY GLUED WALLET SHUT. (WON'T LET YOU TRY TO GET IT OPEN.)

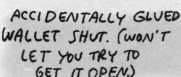

HAS NOTHING BUT A THOUSAND-DOLLAR BILL AND HE'S TAKING IT TO THE ORPHANAGE.

Tuesday 10

Dear Dumb Diary,

Angeline is on to yet *another* charity. This one donates old clothes to people. She asked Anika and Hudson for a contribution, and I was just about to contribute what a huge dipwad she is when Hudson said he thought it was pretty cool of Angeline to work so hard for needy people. And so did Anika, which made Isabella's head nod involuntarily, because that's what her head does when several other people agree on something. (Also Angeline was wearing the barrette again, which may have had some persuasive powers.)

Then Angeline turned to me and said, "You probably got rid of all your old stuff at your garage sale on Sunday, Jamie, so I doubt you have anything to donate."

"Shucks!" I thought. (Actually I thought something much worse, but I will get in huge trouble for writing it, so I'm going to stick with shucks.)

"Shucks! Angeline *did* know it was my house. But she can't be sure it was *my* stuff!" I thought cleverly. Make that *VERY cleverly.*

Jamie Kelly, GIANT- BRAINED Genius GIRL →

I HAVE JUST 3 WORDS FOR REAL GIANT- BRAINED GENIUS GIRLS: BANGS, BANGS, BANGS.

So I said, "No. No. That garage sale was something my mom was doing. None of that stuff was mine. I always selflessly donate my old junk to charities. I'll have a big bag of clothes for you. Right away. Yup, a huge bag."

Pretty good thinking, huh? Except for not having a big bag of clothes. Or even a little bag. Other than that, pretty good thinking.

MY STORY had more HOLES in it than DAD'S OLDEST UNDIES.

ILLEGAL TO SHOW UNDERPANTS THIS HOLEY

BUT YOU HAVE TO ADMIT IT — IT'S NOT THAT HARD TO BELIEVE in BIGFOOT, IS IT?

The teamwork exercise in Phys Ed today was this: the little groups race one another in an exercise called **Sled Dogs**. One person sits on the floor on a towel and grabs on to a broom while the other members of the team drag him or her across the gym. Each person takes a turn on the towel. I guess this is to determine who is good at thinking up an excuse to not have to participate in Phys Ed that day.

WHEEZE HUFF PUFF GRUNT

REAL SLED DOGS BEING TOTALLY EMBARRASSED FOR US

Anyway, Angeline must really be mad at Pinsetti's head, because she distracted me again, which caused me to accidentally hit him in the noggin with the broomstick when I turned to see what Blondewad and Hudson were giggling about this time.

Pinsetti was sort of dazed and spoke a little Egyptian or French or something. Dover yelled at me to be more careful, but I think Pinsetti was faking it, because broomsticks probably break over heads easier than you think.

I also think it didn't help that Isabella was shouting, "Again! Again!" over and over.

Wednesday 11

Dear Dumb Diary,

Today at lunch, Isabella said she'd heard that Angeline had raised $300 for her Walk-A-Thon. They put a sign up by the office. I couldn't believe how much more famous that made her. How famous does she need to be? If it was me, I would be totally satisfied with being partly famous and not have to go making myself famouser all the time.

probably
How
famous
she wants
to be

LOVE
ME

MOST

And all day, Isabella couldn't stop talking about the money. She was like: "Three **HUNDRED** bucks. For a **charity**. Nobody even knows who these people are or anything, and they coughed up three **HUNDRED** buckaroos."

Then she took a bite out of her hot dog and it scared me a little. I don't know why, but to me it looked like she was pretending that the hot dog was the throat of the entire human race.

Isabella came over tonight, and she brought a movie to watch: *Beauty and the Beast*. As it turns out, there is more than one version of this movie, and Isabella did **NOT** bring the excellent cartoon version with the singing teapot and dancing candlestick. She brought some old one with the people speaking French (sounding a lot like head-injury Pinsetti) and you had to read what they were saying at the bottom of the screen.

These are called subtitles, and they are designed to make an irritating movie more irritating. These subtitles stayed on the screen way too long, so I kept reading them over and over, which made it seem like all the characters were repeating themselves like my grandma does — except that at least they didn't go on and on about how they could buy a root beer for a dime when they were kids, which was good I guess, because I'll bet you can really work up a thirst running from dinosaurs.

65 MILLION YEARS AGO, GRANDMA WAS ABOUT MY AGE

Anyway, the message of the movie was about the same, I guess: **Real Beauty** comes from within. **Blah, blah, blah.** But if this was true, instead of bathing suits and nine-inch heels, wouldn't they make the contestants bring their X-rays to the Miss America Pageant?

Thursday 12

Dear Dumb Diary,

    We got a **HUGE** assignment in Phys Ed today. **HUGE!** I can't believe that I ever suggested to Mr Dover that he change the routine. If I had never done that, I would be enjoying my many assorted cramps right now instead of teamwork.

cramps are just like friends...

that don't want you to enjoy yourself.

Here's our big assignment. This is **so** big that Dover is basing **HALF** of our grade on it. Each little group of four gets divided up. One person stands on one side of the gym, and the other three line up across from him or her. Using only a **soup pot**, a **rubber snake** and a **high-heeled shoe**, we have to get a **baby doll** across the gym floor to that fourth member.

We have to get the baby ALL the WAY ACROSS THE GYM

ISABELLA IS NOT THAT GREAT AT DOLL HOLDING

But we can't just walk across the gym floor.
And the baby can't touch it at all. We have to
pretend the floor is full of **crocodiles**. And we
may not simply hurl the baby across, because we're
supposed to pretend it's our precious baby, and
if the fourth member fails to catch it that would
be curtains for baby. Other than that, Dover said,
anything goes.

We have four whole weeks to figure this out,
but if we accomplish the task sooner, and prove to
Dover we can do it, we can just sit around during
gym and watch everybody else work it through.

School is preparing me for
the REAL world with FAKE
BABies AND pretend crocodiles.

So Dover lined us up in our group formations. He said he could walk anywhere in the gym because he has some sort of special resistance to the crocodiles. Then he handed the dolls to the people who are going to be on the left side of the gym.

Angeline took one look at her baby and said, "Mr Dover, something is wrong with our doll."

Dover walked over and looked at the doll and said, "Angeline, I don't see anything wrong with this."

"Well, could you see what Hudson thinks?" she said, and Dover walked over and handed it to Hudson, who was standing on the other side of the gym.

Angeline smiled, looked at Mr Dover, and said, **"We're done."**

PURe SMUGNeSS

There was this moment of silence when our normal, innocent brains had to get up to speed and realize what Angeline had done. She had got the baby across the gym according to the rules, and she had done in twenty seconds what the rest of us were going to need four weeks to do. Plus, she had tricked a teacher to accomplish it, right there in front of everybody.

The applause was deafening. Mr Dover, in the interest of sportsmanship, **HAD** to accept the solution, but then he set a new rule: that none of the rest of us could trick a person to accomplish the task.

SHE TRICKED DOVER

MUNCH

Except for BITING HIS HEAD OFF, there's nothing kids would have respected more.

I spent the rest of the class watching smugly barretted Angeline and Hudson sit over in a corner of the gym laughing and talking while my little group dumbly scratched our dumb butts like dumb apes and came up with nothing.

When class was over and it was time to clean up, I tossed the pot to Pinsetti, who, it turns out, wasn't looking (which was kind of his fault, according to Isabella), and I accidentally hit him right in the exact spot where I had dropped him in Trust Falls, and where I'd broken the broomstick.

He started yelling at me, but Isabella jumped in and said if his head is so sensitive to injury then maybe he should just suck it up and wear a helmet when I'm around. I'm so glad that I have a friend like Isabella, who grew up with terrible mean brothers who made her so cruel and quick to lash out. It really is a blessing.

EVERYBODY SHOULD HAVE A FRIEND AS MEAN AS ISABELLA

I know. I know. Why didn't Pinsetti go nuclear on me? I mean, one time he got in a fight with a kid and messed him up so bad the kid had to eat prescription soup for a month.

I think it's because he had a crush on me once, and the lingering effect of the crush kept his anger subdued.

It's a known science fact that **Crush Enzymes** can stay in your system for up to six years. Love is so powerful that only swallowed gum endures longer.

How Long Things stay with You

♥	After-Effects of Crush.	6 years
	swallowed Gum.	7 years
	Embarrassment of your Dad rapping in front of your friends.	Forever, Dude. Forever.

Friday 13

Dear Dumb Diary,

Angeline came around at lunch today and asked for that big bag of clothes that I lied about and she so rudely believed. I thought about just admitting that I didn't have any clothes for her and, besides, I really don't care that much if the people in Whereheckistan want my old junk. But then Hudson walked up with a paper bag and handed it to her.

"I have some stuff for that clothing charity," he said. And then he said, "I think it's really great what you're doing." And I realized ANGELINE WAS NOT WEARING THE BARRETTE! He was looking at her differently from when she was merely beautiful. Hudson was *impressed* by her generosity. Hudson was seeing the inner Angeline.

Oh, my gosh. It's like *Beauty and the Beast*. Except Angeline is some sort of Beast that has Inner Beauty **and** Outer Beauty, so it's **Beauty and the Beauty.** There is no Beast.

Angeline is like one of those candies that's chocolate on the outside, and when you bite into it there's even better chocolate on the inside. And there's only one of those in the box. And you can't help it if you're born one of those brittle, maple-toffee, old-people flavours.

If you think Angeline made me crazy before this, Dumb Diary, that was nothing. Angeline isn't just beautiful on the outside, she may also be beautiful **ON THE INSIDE**, which means she is much much *much* MUCH *MUCH* **MUCH MUCH** worse.

Beauty is only skin-deep, but hate goes all the way to the bone.

The Beautiful chrysalis opens and the Beautiful caterpillar emerges as A BEAUTIFULLER BUTTERFLY

MAN, I HATE BUGS

So I told Angeline that I had forgotten the bag this morning because I was so busy making posters for my new charity, **Take An Underprivileged Koala To Lunch Day,** that I forgot. Of course, she was interested in the charity, but I told her we were still working out some of the details, like making sure the restaurant had enough booster seats for the koalas.

I know. I know. Another lame lie. But it was all I could think of, and I wouldn't even look at Isabella, who I'm sure was deeply disappointed — yet again — in my lack of inner wickedness.

Saturday 14

Dear Dumb Diary,

I tore up the house this morning. We had *NO* old clothes. Mom's brilliant garage sale strategy had wiped us out. Even Dad's old **way-too-short shorts** were gone.

Just admit it, Dad. You cut them too short.

Isabella wouldn't give me any of her old clothes, because she said that if her clothes went to some mysterious country they could use them to do voodoo against her. You can't really argue this sort of thing with Isabella. She feels pretty strongly about voodoo, having tried to work it several thousand times. But she did have another idea, and face it: **Isabella always has great ideas.**

She said we'd just **pretend** we're working for Angeline's charity. We'll go to a couple of houses of people we know and collect old clothes. It's not really a lie, right? Since we kind of **ARE** working for the charity.

ISaBeLLA DOeSN'T USE PiNS Because She says staples would probably HURT MORE

The first house we went to was Mrs Clawson's. She's the old lady who lives next door to me. We told her about the charity, *blah, blah, blah,* and she gave us a great big bag of old clothes, so I was done in **just one house!** Except that when we got back to my house we found that the entire bag was full of those giant old-lady underpants that look like old army-man parachutes with two big holes shot through them.

Awestruck and sickened

There was **NO WAY** I was going to let Angeline think those were mine, so I gave them to Stinker to eat or bury or whatever he does with stuff like that. He was still mad at me for sitting on him, so I figured that would make us even.

The Cutlers live on the other side of us, so we went there next. They have a couple of girls in college, so I figured the clothes they'd have to donate wouldn't make me look too bad.

Just as Mrs Cutler was handing over a couple of items, Isabella added that we were also collecting donations for **The Juvenile Optometry Federation,** which supplies eyeglasses and such to underprivileged kids. Incredibly, Mrs Cutler handed Isabella five dollars for it.

Isabella was super Happy! She must really love charity.

Isabella said that she got the information about this charity online and I could help her collect for it if I wanted to, so as we made the rounds for the clothes, we also picked up a few bucks here and there for the Juvenile Optometry Federation.

Hooray! Now I have a charity to work for. In your face, Angeline — now I'm as gentle and sweet as you, you pig. And we got almost fifteen dollars in donations already!!

Look! I have as much inner Beauty as BLONDEWAD.

Oooh. I'll bet that animals can magically SENSE IT!

Sunday 15

Dear Dumb Diary,

    Okay. Remember how I didn't know exactly what Stinker would do with a bag of old-lady underpants? Well, this morning, I found out what he would do. He would run outside and, like, **STREW** them across Mrs Clawson's front lawn, from one side to the other, until it looks like her lawn is covered with humongous, billowy mushrooms.

EEEWWWWW!

And of course my first impulse would be to just close the blinds and lie about it, but if Mrs Clawson looked out there and saw her unmentionables being mentioned like crazy she might have a heart attack. There was nothing I could do but run outside before anybody else saw and gather them up.

Not with my hands, of course. With barbecue tongs. I mean, c'mon. Old-lady underpants? **Uck.**

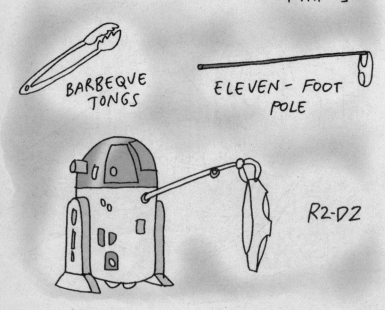

TOOLS YOU MAY NEED TO HANDLE OLD-LADY UNDERPANTS

BARBEQUE TONGS

ELEVEN - FOOT POLE

R2-D2

So I ran over there with a little wastebasket and my tongs, and started picking them up and quickly getting them into the can — hopefully before Mrs Clawson looked out of the window or any neighbours walked past. I had about half of them gathered up when round the corner comes Angeline and about a thousand of her Walk-A-Thonners. Remember when Angeline mentioned the *next* Walk-A-Thon? Turns out it was today.

CAUGHT TONGING THE DAINTIES

Of course Angeline had to stop and say hi and have a good look at the lawn, the tongs, the can and the old-lady underpants. "What are you doing?" she asked.

Dumb Diary, I'm going to level with you. It was not easy to admit the truth to Angeline.

So I didn't.

"Mrs Clawson has a severe allergy to dryers, so every week, I charitably launder her giant horrible underpants and gently lay them out here on the lawn to dry," I said, and at this point I gently tonged one pair of panties and spread it out carefully. "It's a lot of work, and of course a ghastly eyesore, but I do it out of charity."

"Want me to help?" she said, trying to muscle in on my charity. It was fake, but, still, it was mine.

"That's okay," I said, and waved my panty tongs at her until she and the others had walked all the way down the block.

Then I scooped up Mrs Clawson's dainties and threw them in the trash.

It was a close call, Dumb Diary, but I got away with it. No more old-lady underpants for Stinker. Not until Christmas, anyway.

PROBABLY STINKER'S BIG CHRISTMAS DREAM

Monday 16

Dear Dumb Diary,

It's amazing how excited Isabella is over our new charity thing. I told her that I really thought this Juvenile Optometry Federation was going to make us better people and she agreed. In fact, she agreed so much that she even laughed a little.

She's made a sign that she taped up in the hallway at school. We're supposed to get permission to tape things up, but Isabella said that charity flyers are automatically okay.

She said that the government says that anything that promotes better health is also LeGAL to put up.

FOR INSTANCE →

HEY, STINKY, WOULD IT KILL YOU TO TAKE A BATH?

I WILL MAKE HYGIENE MYGIENE

Isabella even made us cute little donation cans to carry around. **It was amazing!** Even the assistant principal coughed up some spare change, probably because he has a soft spot for glasses. He has those kind of ultrapowerful glasses that make it look like he can see the molecules on the moon.

Isabella thinks he might even be able to see in X-RAY with these glasses

He wears ties, But is nice anyway

Isabella says we're up to almost thirty-two dollars, and soon we'll have enough to give to the charity. We can both feel ourselves becoming beautifuller inside.

Soon, our **inner beauty** will be so inflamed that it will rupture through our skin and spew bubbling squirts of beauty all over ourselves and all over the floor that the janitors will have to clean up with their special throw-up sawdust. Doesn't that sound magnificent?

Let's see Angeline's inner beauty match up to that.

Tuesday 17

Dear Dumb Diary,

　　Angeline and Hudson were making me really mad today in Phys Ed with their stupid chatter, so I tried to get my little group to really organize and think up how to safely get our baby across the lake of crocodiles. TUKWNIF (That Ugly Kid Whose Name I Forget) suggested that we put the baby in the pot and slide it across the floor. But I said if the pot tips over, or doesn't make it all the way over there, the baby is crocodile chow.

She has tricked poor Hudson into thinking he's interested in her dumbness.

Pinsetti thought we could cut the baby into pieces and throw those across the gym, since the rules just said that we couldn't throw the baby but didn't say anything about throwing chunks of baby. We decided that the multiple head injuries weren't doing Pinsetti any good.

But somehow this gave Isabella an idea — though she refused to share it with us. She said she was afraid the others would hear us and steal the idea. She said she knows how to do it, but she's keeping it a secret for now. That was just as well, because we could hear the buses pulling up outside, which is sort of our cue to stop working hard, because the school day is almost over.

Oh, yeah. And as I was jerking open the door to run out of the gym, I may have opened it slightly on Pinsetti's face, but he should be used to that by now. He's taken more blows to the head this month than a sturdy piñata at a greedy kid's birthday party.

Wednesday 18

Dear Dumb Diary,

They announced a new fund-raising Jump-Rope-A-Thon event in school today. It's a jump-rope marathon, and you get people to sponsor you based on the number of times you jump over the rope without tripping. The Jump-A-Thon is a week from now, and the money goes to the school, which is finally a pretty good charity, I think. (Maybe they can use the money to buy some new office ladies, since the ones we have now are a little wrinkled and stained.)

TRASH

NICE NEW OFFICE LADY

Hudson asked us if we were going to be participating. Of course, Isabella and I are doing it, but when Angeline walked by and Hudson asked her she choked a bit before she said yes.

That little choke made me think that maybe she's all out of inner beauty. Can that happen? Can you use up your inner beauty? Can you touch it up by swallowing cosmetics?

Thursday 19

Dear Dumb Diary,

Isabella explained her solution to us today in Phys Ed. She made us huddle together so that she could secretly describe it. She was not going to let anybody else have the answer.

When we heard her solution, we just smiled. She **HAD** figured it out, and we decided to try it right after class.

As always, everybody immediately ran out of the gym when the bell rang, and that gave us enough time to attempt Isabella's solution before we demonstrated it in class to Mr Dover.

Isabella is as smart as a teacher and even a little meaner.

We put the pot over the baby's head. Isabella explained that the pot was a safety precaution to protect our baby. I held the rubber snake's tail, and TUKWNIF held its head. Isabella positioned the baby in the middle of the snake body and pulled it back like a slingshot. Isabella is a master aimer because sometimes the best way for her to battle her brothers is to attack them from a distance.

She let the baby go and — *TWANG* — it
easily sailed over the pretend crocodiles and right
into Pinsetti's arms, safe and sound!

We had totally followed the rules. We hadn't
"thrown" the baby. We had *launched* the baby.
Dover is going to give us an **A** for sure.

TWAANNG!

And, to everybody's surprise, I didn't accidentally injure Pinsetti's head today, which I'm sure made him feel better.

But that didn't last long, because when he put his cap on he opened the scab for, like, the third time.

Isabella gently consoled him by telling him that his head injuries are our team's good-luck charm, so Pinsetti should feel proud. Also, she gently yelled at him to quit crying, which I think helped us.

Times when Isabella Yells

To make you stop crying. Or start crying.

To tell you she is unhappy. Or happy.

To whisper a secret to you from across the room.

HEY you LeFt some underpants at my house!

Friday 20

Dear Dumb Diary,

Angeline's picture was in the paper *again.*

And Hudson was the one that brought it to my attention. "Look! Angeline has her picture in the paper again. This time it's for donating all those clothes!"

Angeline walked by and Hudson was all, "Look, Angeline. It's you again."

Angeline pretended to blush. "It's just these charity things. Sooner or later they all wind up in the paper. Sometimes months afterwards. I don't know why I manage to get in the shots so often."

Gosh, hmm. Let's think about that for a moment. **Hmm. Gee.** I can't imagine. It couldn't have anything to do with your unfairly beautiful exterior and your even beautifuller interior, could it?? **Hmm.** No, couldn't be that. **Gosh,** Angeline. It's a real mystery, isn't it?

It's really no wonder that photographers want to shoot her.

I know I would.

Was there a picture of me and Isabella raising money for our charity — The Juvenile Optometry Federation? **(Donations now exceed thirty-five dollars!)** No. Any picture of me getting pledges for the Jump-Rope-A-Thon next Wednesday? **No.** (I'm up to **THREE** pledges, thank you very much. Dad couldn't donate. He said he lost his wallet at a rodeo. Wait a second. I don't remember any rodeo.)

I think Dad's excuse might have been pure bull.

Saturday 21

Dear Dumb Diary,

Today seemed like a great day to do charity. Isabella said that she knew she'd be more beautiful soon, too. We tried to get Jump-A-Thon money from her folks, aunts, uncles, cousins, neighbours, you name it. And we watched those sponsors escalate from three sponsors to a mind-boggling . . .

Seven sponsors.

That's seven sponsors **BETWEEN US.**
Most people pledge a penny a hop. So if Isabella
and I jump rope a hundred times in a row, we may
raise enough money to provide one student with a
box of crayons. Not the box of sixty-four with the
sharpener, of course. Just the box of sixteen, and
not even a good brand, just those waxy ones they
give you at restaurants.

Even though they gave you the crayons, Do NOT Draw cute pictures of the waitress on your placemat.

THE DUMB FAT-BUTTED WAITRESS

She will spill coffee on your Dad which means I didn't get to ORDER DESSERT

Sunday 22

Dear Dumb Diary,

   Isabella came over today to practise jumping rope. We figure that our best strategy is to jump way longer than a hundred jumps. I am an only child, which means that, growing up, I often had nothing better to do than stand out in the driveway by myself and practise jumping rope. Kids with no brothers or sisters usually have a couple of these skills that require a lot of alone practice time.

SKIPPY
SKIPPY
SKIP
SKIP
SKIPPY

As I've tried to explain to you a million times, D. D., Isabella has mean older brothers, so the jump rope was an essential toy for her, as well. Not only is she good at jumping, she has kung fu-like abilities with it. When her brothers hear the sound of the rope whisking on the cement, the hairs on the back of their necks stands up.

No wonder. I've seen her do some pretty scary things with it.

We practised for a long time this afternoon. We're pretty sure we can easily do more than a hundred hops. We might even be able to buy the school as many as two pairs of those small, blunt, dull scissors that you only try to use when somebody else is borrowing the teacher's good scissors. Or maybe we can just buy Margaret a light snack of forty pencils or so.

Other Things OUR School Should BUY

Adorable Uniforms for the female custodians

A Puppy to live inside every locker

DRINKING FOUNTAINS THAT LASER-BEAM PEOPLE THAT SPIT THEIR GUM OUT IN THEM

ZAP

Monday 23

Dear Dumb Diary,

Today, I asked Isabella if she wanted to try to raise more money for the Juvenile Optometry Federation, and she looked at me as though she had never heard of it. Had she forgotten about our charity already?

After a few minutes, it all came back to her and she said that she sent them the money and now they had enough and we can stop raising money.

What Isabella's face does when she can't remember something

Can you believe it? **We totally filled up a charity.** Of course I had to walk over and share this with Hudson, who was being victimized by having lunch with Angeline.

"We filled our charity all the way to the top," I said. "Full up. **COMPLETELY** charitized them. Yup. We charitized the crud out of those kids."

How BEAUTIFUL ARE we? Those far-sighted little brats are probably DROWNING IN MONeY! YAY.

But Angeline did not look wounded by the **Huge Club of Pure Charity** that I had just hit her in the face with. She looked sort of, well, *impressed.* And so did Hudson. Maybe some of my inner beauty was starting to leak out? It probably wasn't the barrette, because I'm still not sure I'm getting the most out of this thing, and I don't think I'm remembering to wear it all the time.

GORGEOUS

PRETTY

SLIGHTLY CUTE

PLAIN

UGLY

WOOF

BEAUTY

BEAUTY

MY inNeR Beauty is on the Rise!

Tuesday 24

Dear Dumb Diary,

    What the heck! We were all ready to do our final test and fling our precious baby through the air, but Dover said we had to help get the gym set up for the Jump-Rope-A-Thon, which is tomorrow after school. I was pretty upset until I realized that this meant that Anika, Pencilmunch, Blondewad and Hudson had to help.

Butt has gone totally flat from non-stop lazy sitting on the gym floor →

There was not too much to do, really. Hang a few banners, get the tables and chairs set up for the judges, open the doors and windows to help get out the odour of **kid stink**.

Dover could easily have done this without our help, but some teachers tend to think that the kids should do their physical work for them, like farm animals, except even a little grosser in the case of Margaret, who did not miss the chance to sneak a couple of secret munches on one of the pencils from the judges' table.

I don't want to say she's still eating a lot of pencils, but when she farts I swear you can almost see a little puff of sawdust.

Wednesday 25

Dear Dumb Diary,

Jump-Rope-A-Thon day!!!!!!!!!!
School was normal. That's how it started, anyway. And then, like everything that starts normal, it became abnormal.

Right after school, just before we went to the gym, Isabella came out of the bathroom and walked right into a wall. When she turned towards me, I saw that she was not wearing her glasses any more. And, when she got closer, I could see that her eyes had turned green. Green like a jelly bean.

"Isabella! What happened to your eyes?" I said.

"I got contacts," she said. "Just put 'em in. Cool, huh?"

"Where did you get the money for contacts?" I said, knowing that her parents would not have approved, *and* that Isabella has a very hard time saving money.

"The Juvenile Optometry Federation," she said. "Plus I had a few bucks saved up." And she laughed that kind of laugh that psychopaths laugh when they have you cornered in the basement.

THE WEIRD EYES COMPLETED THE PSYCHOPATH EFFECT NICELY

I felt sick. Isabella had faked the charity. And I had helped her. "Isabella! Our inner beauty! What have you done?"

"Look," she said, "they're IN my eyes, right? And they're beautiful. **Bang: Inner Beauty.** I didn't have enough for the tinted ones, so I coloured them myself. I think I may have used a little too much green marker on them, and I might have wrecked the left one. If you get some, you should take them out of your eyes before you colour them."

ONLY ISABELLA AND SPACE ALIENS ARE CAPABLE OF DOING THIS

They were practically stolen, kind of. But there was nothing I could do, and Isabella knew it. I had helped her, so if I ratted her out I'd be in just as much trouble as she would be. We had faked out the principal, which is like faking out the president. All I could do was lead her to the gym. She was almost blind.

Lots of kids showed up to participate in the Jump-Rope-A-Thon. I didn't see Angeline right away, which is odd, because she is so into these things. Mr Dover and a few other teachers were the judges, but a couple of them were late, so Mr Dover asked if Isabella and I could help by counting other kids' jumps first, and then do our jumping last. Since we're totally jumping experts, we said okay.

As the participants did their jumps, we'd record the number and drop the sheets off with the judges. Isabella had to count by the sound of the jumps, of course, because her vision was all blurry from her contacts.

Margaret and TUKWNIF were really good jumpers: no doubt that **Time-Alone-To-Practise** thing helped, and jump-rope handles are big, juicy, delicious knobs of wood, and we all know how that appeals to Margaret. (Never caught her but I'm sure she got in a little **gnaw-time**.)

After a while, we got down to the last few jumpers, and Angeline slid into the gym. She had this look on her face I had never seen before.

She called me over, and she was sort of panicked. I wished that Isabella could have seen it, but her eyes had started to roll independently like a chameleon's. (Marker poisoning?)

When Angeline had me alone, she — are you ready for this? — **CONFESSED.** She was almost crying when she told me that she can't jump rope by herself. Hardly at all. See, it's like I said before. Jumping rope is a skill you practise when you spend lots of time alone. Angeline, being totally popular and always busy, has never had time to master it.

Ha-ha! I just knew that if I lived long enough I'd discover the **BAD SIDE** of intense popularity. You never get any "me time". It's always "we time". You're followed everywhere. Maybe even into the bathroom. Even your **wee** time is **we** time.

Yup, it was a tragic moment for Angeline. A wonderfully tragic moment. It was so sad I almost burst out laughing.

But the moment didn't last. She showed me her pledge sheet. Angeline had more than a **HUNDRED** sponsors. She may be bad at jumping rope, but she is great at collecting for charities. Every time that rope went round, Angeline would make, like, ten bucks or something for the school.

TONS OF CASH

It was so wonderful! All that money and she was going to blow it because she couldn't work a stupid jump rope. So much for your inner beauty, Ang. Wait till everybody finds out how you let the whole school down!

The school . . .

PLINK!

NOOO! The School!!! Why did I even have to think about the school?!

If I let Angeline fail, it would be a huge blow to her — her popularity, her inner beauty, her smug barrette skills, and her evil power over Hudson.

But it would also be a huge blow to the school. Nobody else had anywhere near as many sponsors. I had seen the sheets.

Without This Money, The School COULD FAce Terrible Cuts Like These:

The orchestra could get reduced to kazoos only

They might have to stop giving teachers free coffee

The cafeteria might switch Meat LoAf from Thursdays to seven DAYS A WEEK AND make us come in for lunch on weekends!

And as I looked into Angeline's eyes I saw that she was sad. Like real sad. Not sad like when a beagle can't scratch the barrette off his ears, but sad like when you know you're letting everybody down. And she made my inner beauty squirt out of me until I was standing in a puddle of my own loveliness. I had created a monster — a beast. And it was me. I was a real **Beauty of a Beast** and a **Beast of a Beauty**.

I went over and asked Dover if the jumpers had to hold the jump rope themselves, or if they could just jump it. Because if they had to hold it that wouldn't be fair to people with no hands, like pirates. Dover looked in the rules and said that the person only had to jump — somebody else *could* twirl the rope.

That's right. Somewhere there is somebody who is such A **HUGE NERD** that he wrote a jump-rope rulebook.

I told Isabella that I wanted her to help me twirl the rope for Angeline. Angeline had way more pledges than we had, and this was the only right thing to do for the sake of the charity.

Isabella said, "Forget it," and she wanted to storm off, but, her vision being what it was, she could only wander off aimlessly.

So I got up real close into her face, and I made my voice as low and as dangerous as hers, and I said to her, "Isabella, either you do this or I'll tell your parents and everybody how you got the money for your contact lenses. You'll be grounded until you graduate from college."

where did all that inner beauty go?

I could hardly believe I had said it. Isabella's eyes started to tear up a little, but it wasn't because I had hurt her feelings. And, it wasn't because her contacts were bugging her. It was because she was **moved**.

See, Isabella is a master of blackmail. It's one of the horrible abilities her brothers' cruelty has forced her to develop. After all these years, Isabella could see that I had finally learned something wicked from her. She was touched by my **Inner Ugly,** which to her is exactly like **Inner Beauty** — so much that it moved her to tears.

"Okay," she said.

Angeline *DOES* know how to jump rope if somebody else twirls it. And, actually, she can jump pretty well. Not like Isabella, and not at all like me, but she jumped for a long time, and we raised a bunch of money for the school. This was probably going to be her biggest jackpot yet, and her inner beauty and fame were going to skyrocket off the charts.

I was furious and delighted at the same time.

Why can Angeline only jump this way?

Maybe because she's used to playing in groups, and she needs both hands to keep her hair out of her eyes

Thursday 26

Dear Dumb Diary,

My arms were killing me when I woke up this morning. You use different muscles when you twirl a rope for somebody else, and I felt like I had a huge charley horse in my shoulders. Can you get a charley horse in your shoulders?

Anyway, this was worse. More like a charley *moose*.

why do they call a bad thigh pain "charley Horse"? why not "Jane Donkey" or "BoB the Penguin"?

Isabella wanted to do our solution for Dover in Phys Ed class today. I told her that my arms were killing me, and I tried to talk her out of it, but she was sure she wanted to go for it, and you know how she gets.

We waited until towards the end of the class so we could review our solution and make sure it would go as planned. We could hear the buses starting to pull up, so we had to move quickly.

Dover watched as we loaded the baby into the snake slingshot. Isabella started to pull it back, but her contact lenses were bugging her eyes and she was having a hard time aiming. I could tell she was off target, but my arms hurt so bad I couldn't compensate for it, and when she let the baby go, it wasn't exactly heading in the right direction.

Pinsetti probably could have caught it, but a month of head injuries had him spooked, and he ducked, so our baby, with the big metal pot on its head, smashed right through the window.

Then it rolled down the little hill outside the gym, off the kerb and under the wheel of one of the buses as it was pulling up. We looked out just in time to see the bus roll over it and leave a big, dirty, baby pancake on the road.

This is about as BAD AS A BABY'S DAY CAN GO

I don't think Dover even knew what to say. The baby would have had a better chance for survival with the crocodiles. All Dover did was shake his head slowly and walk away. I guess we were failing.

SQUOOSHING A BABY UNDER A BUS IS GOING TO GET YOU AN "F" IN ALMOST ANY CLASS.

I could hardly bear to look at Hudson. And I knew that Angeline was going to be laughing her head off. Not only had we not saved the baby, it looked as though maybe the baby had done something to make us really, really angry. But Angeline wasn't laughing. She was motioning me over to her.

For a second, I thought maybe she wanted to laugh at me close-up

She leaned in close and whispered to me: "Sacrifice." I don't think I would have known what she meant before. But now, since I have lots of inner beauty, I suddenly understood.

"Mr Dover?" I said. "There's more." I quickly gathered everybody's dolls and handed them to Isabella, Pinsetti and TUKWNIF. Then I walked into the centre of the gym.

I announced, "While the crocodiles are busy eating me, the rest of my team will quickly sneak everybody's babies safely across the gym floor."

Mr Dover looked astonished. "Jamie, you're going to let the crocodiles eat you? Doesn't that mean you fail?" he asked.

"I already failed," I said. "But now everybody else passes. And ahead of schedule. So they get next week off, right?"

Dover smiled. He even clapped a couple of times. He said to the whole class, "She's right. The only solution to this problem was for one member to give up everything for the rest of the team. During Trust Falls and Sled Dogs, one person counted on the group. In this exercise, the group counts on one person. You got it, Jamie! A plus."

After class, Hudson and I talked and laughed on our way to the lockers. Angeline passed us and said hello. I said hi back, but Hudson never even saw her. I guess her inner beauty is no match for mine.

I really don't know why I didn't start having any inner beauty before this. It's really way easier than monkeying around with a barrette.

And look - Now Angeline is some sort of invisible rodent girl →

Friday 27

Dear Dumb Diary,

Never do anything, ever. That's my new motto.

This morning I was feeling pretty good about my new inner beauty. And Isabella was feeling pretty good about her new contacts. She was telling Margaret all about them, but I could see that she thought she was talking to me. I think I'd better take Isabella back to the eye doctor and get those contacts fixed.

HOW ISABELLA SEES THE WORLD NOW

ME   MARGARET   STINKER'S BUTT

Angeline was at her locker today, and right above it was a sign the school had put up that said, CONGRATULATIONS, ANGELINE! YOU RAISED $600 FOR THE JUMP-ROPE-A-THON. A NEW STATE RECORD! But Angeline wasn't all glowing like she usually is when she accomplishes more fame for herself. In fact, she seemed a little sad.

THE NORMAL GLOW OF PERFECTNESS

DIPPED IN SADNESS SAUCE

What is this? Why do I have to feel this way?? **Is this the Ugly Side-Effect of Beauty?** Having to think about how other people feel? Anyway, Hudson came up to me and started talking, and I could see Angeline's huge, horrible, beautiful, bright Windex-blue eyes glimmering like a blue-eyed blonde puppy whose head is clamped in a tightening vice. (Why do I think of these things?)

Hudson was there, practically wading up to his waist in my gushing inner beauty.

But then something beautiful inside crawled up my throat and out my mouth and said this:

"You know, Hudson, it was Angeline who helped me solve that baby-and-the-crocodile puzzle yesterday. I would never have thought of making that sacrifice without her."

And then Hudson smiled at Angeline. Who could blame him? The ol' inner beauty plus outer beauty was a pretty delicious parfait.

GAGGING ON YOUR OWN BEAUTY IS WORSE than GAGGING ON ALMOST ANYTHING ELSE

GAKK

I looked up at Angeline's Jump-Rope-A-Thon sign and then locked eyes with Angeline. I tried to broadcast "Fair is fair" with my eyes, and I guess she got the message, because she said to Hudson:

"Well, as long as we're being totally honest, Jamie here helped me with the Jump-Rope-A-Thon. Without her, I probably could never have raised a single dollar."

shouldn't there be a law about how long your eyelashes can be?

OCEAN OF PURE BEAUTY

Then Hudson turned to me again. I should be required to have a lifeguard posted on my head, because now he was *drowning* in my inner beauty. I mean, seriously, I was looking pretty incredible. C'mon, even Angeline knew she was no match for me now. And I didn't even have the barrette in.

Do you want to know how I **KNOW** she knew it? Because the next thing she did was pull out a copy of today's paper.

OCEAN OF PURE BEAUTY

"Jamie's picture is in the paper," she told Hudson. And she was right. The picture was from the Walk-A-Thon. Not the first one, when Angeline walked past our garage sale. But the *second* one, when she saw me and Mrs Clawson's old-lady underpants. Remember how I told you that Angeline's charity junk always winds up in the papers?

I hardly even noticed this guy

AND HIS CAMERA

Here's how the picture looked, with Angeline's jillion-dollar smile and me with a tongful of hag panties:

The caption was something like: "Well-known charity participant pauses during Walk-A-Thon to watch girl play with elder's underpants."

Hudson read it and then looked at me as though I had been *eating* the underpants. I tried to say something. But words kind of fail you at a moment like that. I mean, it *was* me in the picture and, even though I wasn't playing, what I was doing wasn't much better. **My inner beauty was rapidly being replaced with inner weirdness.**

Angeline and Hudson walked away laughing and talking. Angeline looked back over her shoulder, and it seemed as if she was sending me a message like: "Look, it's not my fault you were photographed pantifying a yard in broad daylight when a photographer walked past."

She's right. I guess it wasn't her fault. Not really. But it wasn't exactly my fault, either. There should be somebody to blame, right? I mean all the time. There should be somebody and it's just their job to be blamed.

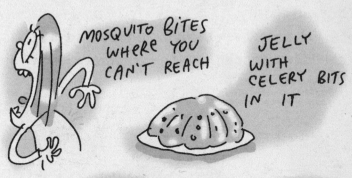

WE NEED TO BE Able to BLAME SOMEBODY FOR:

MOSQUITO BITES WHERE YOU CAN'T REACH

JELLY WITH CELERY BITS IN IT

NOT LETTING US HAVE KOALAS AS PETS, BECAUSE, HONEY, THOSE THINGS **WANT** TO BE CUDDLED BIG TIME

Saturday 28

Dear Dumb Diary,

I went with Isabella and her dad to get her contacts fixed today. She told her dad that she had saved all the money up and he said he was going to buy them for her on her birthday, anyway.

They have a little collection box at the optometrist's office for a charity that really and truly does help underprivileged kids get glasses. I put thirty bucks in to make up for most of the money that Isabella and I had collected for her made-up charity.

I had to. Even though it doesn't make up for Isabella lying about it in the first place, I knew I did the right thing.

Isabella got new contacts, but she said they bothered her eyes even more than the old ones, and by the time we got back to her house, she whispered to me that she was going back to her glasses. It may have had something to do with the pictures in the optometrist's office of gorgeous models wearing glasses.

NOW ISABELLA PROBABLY THINKS HER GLASSES MAKE HER A SUPERMODEL

I had made forty-five dollars off the garage sale, but even after the eye doctor's I still had fifteen bucks left, so that was still pretty decent for a bunch of old junk.

Until Mrs Clawson called. She had seen the picture in the paper also, and said if I was just going to play with her underpants then she wanted them back. Since I had thrown them out, Mom confiscated the remaining fifteen bucks to buy her new ones.

underpants rage

And, worse, she made me go with her to buy the replacements. I felt bad about Mrs Clawson's ghastly giant bloomers, so I gave Mom an extra ten dollars from my piggy bank to buy her some nicer ones. I suggested a thong, but then my stomach churned a little, so I suggested something flowery instead. Pretty charitable, of me, huh? Maybe I *do* have inner beauty after all.

ONE SECRET VICTORIA SHOULD KEEP

MRS CLAWSON IN THONG TOO HORRIBLE TO SHOW EVEN IN MY OWN DIARY

When we got home, there was a big envelope on the front porch addressed to me. It was from Angeline. Inside was **Big Ol' Pudding-Stain Duck Shirt** and a note, which said:

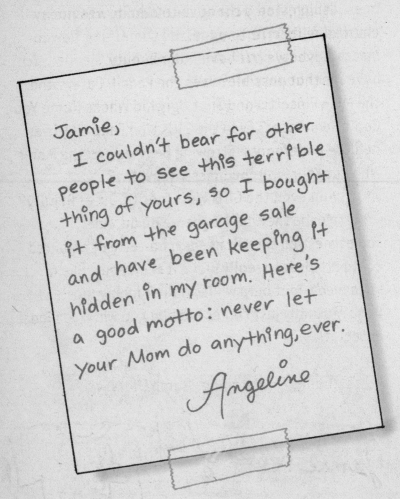

Jamie,

I couldn't bear for other people to see this terrible thing of yours, so I bought it from the garage sale and have been keeping it hidden in my room. Here's a good motto: never let your Mom do anything, ever.

Angeline

It looks like Angeline bought this grimy thing at our garage sale and hid it from the other Walk-A-Thonners, which, I have to admit, was pretty darn charitable.

Which, now *you* have to admit, was pretty charitable for *me* to admit.

Maybe we *all* have Inner Beauty.

Is that possible? Even the Pencil-Eaters and the Mike Pinsettis and That Ugly Kid Whose Name You Can't Remember? Even the Girls Who Fake Charities, and the Underpants-Strewing Beagles and the Moms Who Put Your Wretchedness On Display?

And even the Girls With Tons Of Outer Beauty?

Maybe they do. Maybe we all do. And sometimes you think it needs a barrette or coloured contact lenses to really make it shine, but, like a huge meat-loaf burp while you're running laps, Beauty usually just comes bubbling up when you least expect it.

Thanks for listening, Dumb Diary.

Jamie Kelly

Want to enhance your inner beauty for real?

These organizations can always use help. Ask your parents or teachers how to get involved with these charities or others:

OneSight

British Red Cross

Doctors Without Borders

Make-A-Wish Foundation

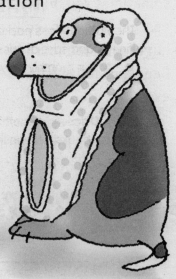

Bright and shiny and sizzling with fun stuff ...

puffin.co.uk

WEB FUN

UNIQUE and exclusive digital content!
Podcasts, photos, Q&A, Day in the Life of, interviews
and much more, from Eoin Colfer, Cathy Cassidy,
Allan Ahlberg and Meg Rosoff to Lynley Dodd!

WEB NEWS

The **Puffin Blog** is packed with posts and photos from
Puffin HQ and special guest bloggers. You can also sign up
to our monthly newsletter **Puffin Beak Speak**

WEB CHAT

Discover something new EVERY month –
books, competitions and treats galore

WEBBED FEET

(Puffins have funny little feet and
brightly coloured beaks)

Point your mouse our way today!

It all started with a Scarecrow.

Puffin is seventy years old.
Sounds ancient, doesn't it? But Puffin has never been
so lively. We're always on the lookout for the next big
idea, which is how it began all those years ago.

Penguin Books was a big idea from the mind of
a man called Allen Lane, who in 1935 invented
the quality paperback and changed the world.
**And from great Penguins, great Puffins grew,
changing the face of children's books forever.**

The first four Puffin Picture Books were hatched in 1940 and the
first Puffin story book featured a man with broomstick arms called
Worzel Gummidge. In 1967 Kaye Webb, Puffin Editor, started the
Puffin Club, promising to **'make children into readers'**.
She kept that promise and over 200,000 children became
devoted Puffineers through their quarterly instalments of
Puffin Post, which is now back for a new generation.

Many years from now, we hope you'll look back and
remember Puffin with a smile. **No matter what your age
or what you're into, there's a Puffin for everyone.**
The possibilities are endless, but one thing is for sure:
whether it's a picture book or a paperback, a sticker book
or a hardback, **if it's got that little Puffin
on it – it's bound to be good.**